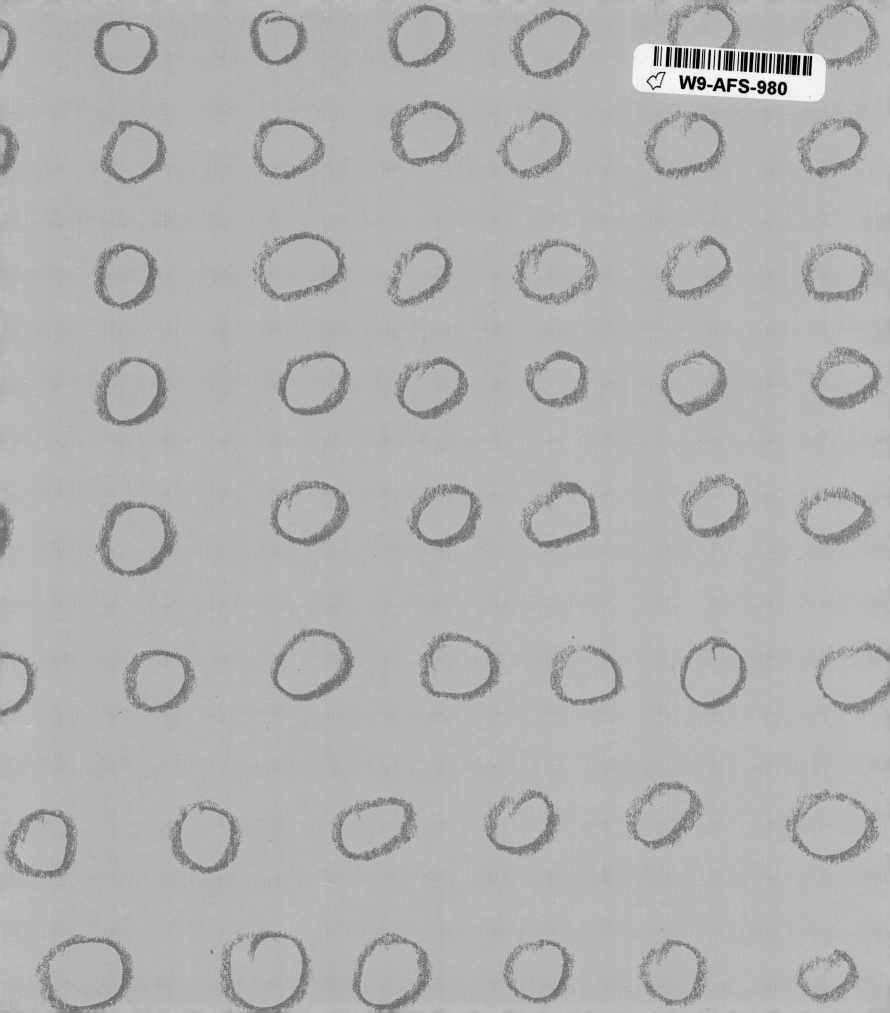

  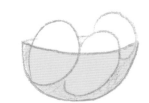 

  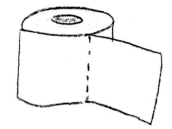

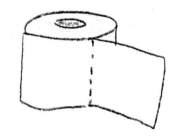

For Armando

First published in 2016 by Child's Play (International) Ltd
Ashworth Road, Bridgemead, Swindon SN5 7YD, UK

Published in USA by Child's Play Inc
250 Minot Avenue, Auburn, Maine 04210

Distributed in Australia by Child's Play Australia Pty Ltd
Unit 10/20 Narabang Way, Belrose, Sydney, NSW 2085

Text and illustrations copyright ©2016 Aurora Cacciapuoti
The moral right of the author/illustrator has been asserted

ISBN 978-1-84643-755-7
L141015CPL04167557

Printed in Heshan, China

1 3 5 7 9 10 8 6 4 2

A catalogue record of this book
is available from the British Library

www.childs-play.com

BAKING WITH DAD

AURORA CACCIAPUOTI

Today is a special day because...

...I am baking with Dad!

We already have all the ingredients.
It's important to choose them carefully!

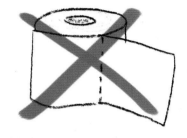

Let's start.

Next, flour.

LOTS of it!

Then, we need
butter and milk, right?

We'll need lots of fruit
to finish off our creation!

Be patient. Let the magic begin!

Time to decorate!

Ding - dong!

Quick! Quick!

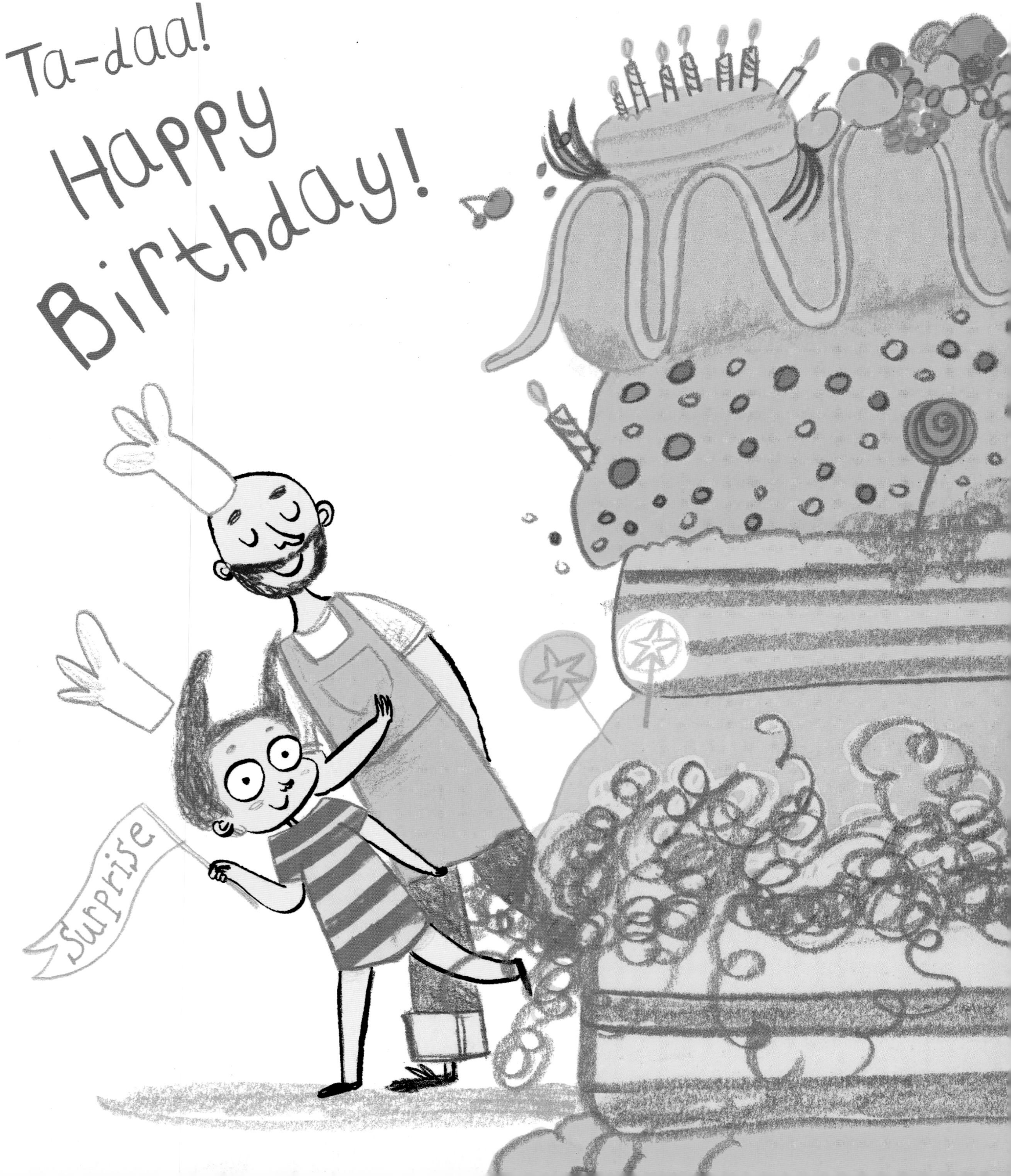
Ta-daa!
Happy Birthday!
Surprise

"Dad, are we going to bake again next week?"

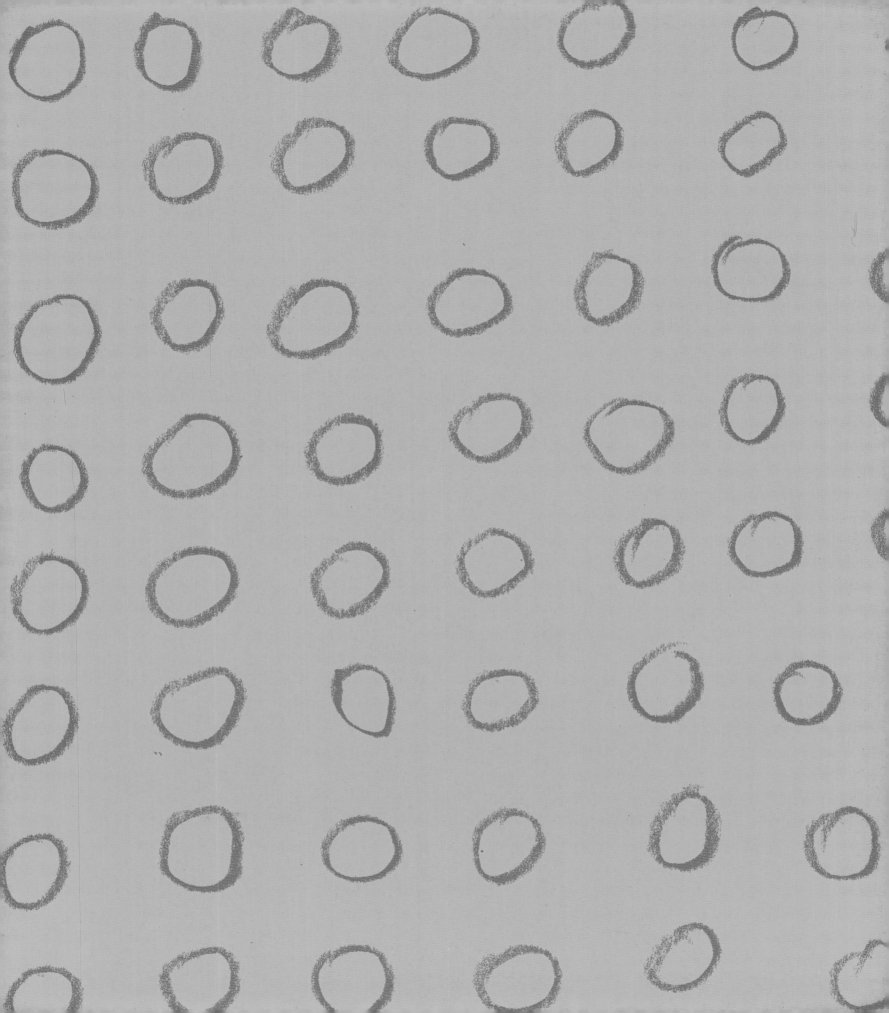